# Bramble Bear

## Can I help?

by Geoffrey Alan

illustrated by Pamela Storey

BRIMAX·NEWMARKET·ENGLAND

"Can I help?" Bramble asks his mother, who is having a baking morning in the kitchen.

"Yes, please," she smiles. "Fetch me the flour from the cupboard. Then you can wash up for me."

Bramble reaches for the big bag of flour. But it is much heavier than he thinks.

He drops it. WHUMP! Flour bursts out everywhere in a dusty, white cloud. Bramble is covered in flour, too. Now he is a very white bear.

"I'm sorry," he sighs. "I was only trying to be helpful."

"You have given me more work," says Bramble's mother. "Now I will have to clean everything – including you!" Bramble has to change. Afterwards, he goes into the garden, where his father is digging.
"Can I help?" he asks.

"You could dig up some weeds for me," puffs his father. He stretches his back, then rubs it. "You know which are weeds, don't you?"

"Yes," Bramble nods. "Just leave it to me!"

"Very well," replies Bramble's father. "I will go indoors for a cup of coffee."

"Now I will show father just how helpful I can be," grins Bramble. He picks up the garden fork and begins to dig. Soon the wheelbarrow is full.
"I've finished!" Bramble calls.
"I will come and have a look," replies his father.
But when he walks into the garden, he stops and stares.
"Oh, no!"

"You have dug up my prize flowers!" groans Bramble's father.

"B . . .but I thought they were weeds," says Bramble, quietly.

Bramble's father takes the garden fork and starts to lift things out of the wheelbarrow with it.

"I will have to plant all these again," he says.

Bramble begins by picking up his clothes and putting them in the wardrobe. He even folds them neatly first. Shortly, all his toys are packed in a wooden chest.

"That leaves the books," says Bramble.

There are lots of books scattered under his bed.

Bramble picks them up and
goes to put them on the shelf.
But he holds too many at once.
He drops some and tries to
catch them.
Bramble loses his balance and
falls back on to his bed.
CRASH! the bed collapses.
Bramble is not hurt. But his
mother and father come
rushing in.

"Don't tell me!" groans his mother. "You were trying to help again."

"I will have to mend the bed," frowns his father.

Bramble decides to be really helpful and go for a walk. He has not gone far when he sees two young rabbits pointing up at a tree.

"Our kite is stuck on that branch," they tell Bramble. "I will climb up and get it for you," he says, eagerly. Carefully, he climbs up and gets closer to the kite. He pulls himself farther and farther along the branch. The kite is hooked on the very end of it.

"I can't quite reach the kite," thinks Bramble. So he shakes the branch and the kite falls down.

"Thank you. *Thank you*," call the rabbits happily.

"Glad to be of help," says Bramble. Then he mutters under his breath, "At last!"

The two rabbits run off,
pulling their kite on a string.
Bramble grins. "Just wait until
I tell mother and father."
He starts to climb down. But he
cannot turn around!
"I'm stuck!" he groans. He calls
the rabbits back and they fetch
his father, with a ladder.
"So much for being a helpful
bear. Now I'm the one who
needs help!"

# Say these words again

| | |
|---|---|
| morning | chest |
| flour | shelf |
| garden | mend |
| weeds | kite |
| stares | branch |
| prize | string |
| mess | ladder |